Published by Ad Hoc Fiction.
www.AdHocFiction.com

Purchasing Information:
Paperback available from www.AdHocFiction.com
E-book available from all usual outlets.

Printed in the United Kingdom.
First Printing 2020.

ISBN paperback 978-1-912095-48-3
ISBN e-Book 978-1-912095-21-6

STORMBRED

by

Eleanor Walsh

Contents

His Name was 'Dreams'

I swim to the beach, dragging him in with my arm around his neck. A coiled wave uncurls, delivers us onto the stones and then retreats, leaving us on our sides in the seaweed like a couple rendered unconscious after a night of drinking. Rolling him over, I wrench his head back and scoop seaweed from his mouth. I pound on his chest so that banners of seawater leap from his nostrils. Stones embed in my knees as I kneel to exhale between his cold lips, my wet hair hangs over his face like kelp. Again, I pummel his chest and feel one of his ribs crack. His tongue lolls and his eyes click open. He's cold. I rest the side of my face on his chest, listening for a heartbeat over the knocking of my own pulse. Overhead, the warblers pule and plummet. I give up as the sun heaves itself from the sea.

"Son of a *bitch*."

Sitting back on my heels, the dawn wind burns my ears and cuts through my salt-wet boiler suit. Sand fleas nip my bare ankles. His lower lip trembles in the wind. The April sky is grey webbed on top of grey: an iris over the bare bones of the sea. I don't try to close his eyes, knowing they will unbutton again. I get to my feet and strain to lift the boulder of his body. His pink tongue pokes through his teeth. As I throw him over my shoulder, seawater from his lungs drains over me, warming me a little. My collar chafes at my throat. I crunch up the beach, tottering under the weight, towards the coast path that leads to the farmhouse balancing on the cliff like a wet pebble. Behind me, the sea retains the bones of winter, and weakly I long for summer and the arrival of blackberries.

Fifth sheep to drown this month. Longing for another home drives them insistently from our paddocks to the sea.

Leonela, let me give you some advice. When I am sleeping and you find yourself in a new country and on the shore with a body, drag him onto the stones but leave him in the cold. I know you will want to bring the body with you, because you see yourself in this body and this body could have been you. But ask yourself how you will carry the weight of him, how you will manage the door to the house with no hands, whereabouts you will kneel to drop this body without allowing the stone of his head to make an unbearable sound on the tiles. Don't think about the way the body has returned, slick, to the state of birth when you wrenched it into this world. Don't think about the bodies that came before, the ones you pulled from rubble. Leave him – because when you arrive – the country will feel closed to you. You will be on the outside looking in, pressed up against it, looking for a way into it, but you will not find your way in until you are able to let go of the body and come alone up the ladder to where I am sleeping. We will fold our arms around each other and together we will face the reality of the body and what it means. In death, we will name him *Dreams* as if he, and our lives up until this moment, never really happened at all.

The Girl from Another Ocean

I leave uncooked porridge oats on the window ledge but the warblers don't come. Lying across the draining board to look at the sky, then back into the kitchen, I try to see if there's something deterring them, but everything seems as it always does. Mine and Pa's chairs at the kitchen table, and the third that's been empty for years. A flower vase, dusty from disuse. The low table that Pa made to put his Bible on, crowded with empty cider bottles. The sofa that Pa sleeps on with its blanket folded and the pillow propped up and doubling as a cushion. By the door is the binbag full of exercise books that was returned to me three months ago, sent here after it was agreed by everyone that it was best that I didn't return to school. Perhaps it's the hint of stale Skreach cider on the air. I shove the window open further to let the weak sea breeze in.

The warblers are feeble this year: no more than feather and exposed nerve. They move like slants of light. They've arrived early to an unseasonably warm April after sensing the war and flying over the Balkan Peninsula without stopping.

Leonela, you'll be waking to human sounds, no hint of music or chatter outside your window. I wonder what war sounds like. I'll admit it: I barely glanced at your photo in the advertising campaign in the newspaper that asked for donations.

Can you help women like Leonela?

The bones in my arms were still knitting together, so painfully that I sweated, and I had taken a double dose of Tramadol, retreated to the attic where I slept on a dinghy that doubled as a bed, and dreamed. Usually I wake from dreams with nothing more than a lingering sense of unease, but this time I remembered clearly that I was ankle deep in rotting seaweed on the beach and was seized by the urge to swim, further than before, further than people had been, further than warblers had flown, further than animals had drowned until I reached a dinghy identical to mine, where you lay, slippery and unconscious as if newborn. With a rope around my hands, I brought you in by swimming, beached you on the shore under the farmhouse. Breathed into you. The water that I sucked from your lungs tasted different, from another ocean.

On waking I had checked the newspaper again. Beneath your photo, the article saying that refugees were fleeing camps by boat, by cobbled-together rafts even, that they were washing up on beaches in Italy and Albania, showing up in nearby villages looking for shelter. Italy was beginning to turn them away.

I showed your photo in the paper to Pa. The birch twig of your arm raised. Your left hand – wrecked from a brief lifetime of heat and grease in a kitchen – pressed against your right eye to scrub away tears. Bones as thin as smoke, your exposed eye fox-like, your ears too, fox-like through the monsoon of your hair. Only your lips betrayed a sob, wrinkling like the surface of the ocean. Your headscarf had unravelled, hanging off one shoulder. My hand twitched with the urge to reach for the scarf, to wrap it again around your head for you, tucking in your hair.

Pa didn't even look up, his unshaven face resting in his hand that held a cigarette smoked down to his fingertips, and he said that Britain couldn't afford to get involved in whatever Botswana had got itself into.

"*Bosnia*, for fuck's sake," I said, ripping your photo out of the newspaper and folding it. I retaliated to Pa's indifference to your picture by telling him that a fifth sheep drowned early in the morning. He flicked his cigarette butt into the vase that once held sheep's-bit and sea-thrift flowers. Before the barn fire, Pa made a stargazy pie every week. Now, rolling shortcrust is too difficult for him. Now, it's whole baked potatoes. Huge saucepans of rice or porridge that sit on the stove for days. No butter, no sugar, no oil.

Leonela – there'll be no drastic change on this fleck of headland to announce your arrival – no unusual choreography from the warblers or crescendo of tempest from the sea. No blossom of thunder or congregation of raincloud. Only the tepid sun slugging itself from the usual sea, only the usual sea sulking beneath a slab of grey. Frost icing the sheep paddocks. So the pill-eyed lambs will come as expected. The familiar sluice of blood and piss, the dip of iodine and unblocking teat and first sputtering squall, until one morning there'll be your outline on the horizon, no more than sound at first – then silhouette – then the unmistakable swipe of an orange dinghy brought in by a repentant sea, where I'll be waiting.

Fallen Stock

Pa is having one of his bad days. It's a Friday so he sends me to Mrs T's shop to deposit a cheque to the electric company, so that if it bounces, we won't be cut off over the weekend. He's supposed to call the local school to ask about me sitting my GCSEs there, but he goes back to sleep on the sofa. In the paper there's a photo of Bosnian refugees sitting on plastic sacks in a camp, while a stooped woman cooks in a pan balanced on bricks. Mud rises in girls' dresses like the tide.

I carry our last sack of 'Hogget Nuts' out in the wheelbarrow, but my arms have lost their strength and I tip it over in the sludge in the gateway, spilling most of them. A couple of ewes approach, sniff at them, and turn away sighing. Their lips and nostrils have grown hard and black with scabs, their long pig-ears droop. One ewe's entire fleece hangs off her and drags along in the mud. She bellows at me across the field like a mad woman shedding her clothes.

The lambs are due 7-in-1 jabs and need to be drenched for worms, but they're no more than fleece over kindling-bone, their skulls wobbling on their ailing bodies. They won't survive a drenching. I change the ear tags on the ewes that had all stillborns this season, marking them out for slaughter. One ewe is foaming at the mouth, but she bucks me off when I try to pin her to look into her throat. *Teasy as'n'adder,* Pa would have called her. Her over-sized muscles balloon over her bones. My arms turn blue with the effort.

Harper from the hunt kennel pulls up in her Ma's jeep. She's been collecting our fallen stock for their dogs since she got her driver's license a month ago. I'm in the yard with my knees clamped around one of the lambs, using a headtorch and tweezers to pick an infestation of ticks from inside the pink map of her ear. I drop each one onto the concrete and squish them under my thumb, enjoying the jets of blood that squirt from their swollen-pea bodies. The lamb snorts at the smell of her own blood and her eyes go back and forth like a metronome.

Harper swings herself out of the driver's seat. Her hair is stiffened to straw from bleaching and she wears thick makeup to cover a raised smattering of acne. Her almond eyes are clogged with eyeliner and she has a ring through the middle of her nose that obscures the thin white scar over her lip. Plastic bangles clack up and down her arms. She glances at the struggling lamb and the blood drying on the concrete, and then looks at me without smiling.

"Hi Ruby."

"Ticks," I say, by way of explanation. She wrinkles her nose.

"What have you got for me?" she asks, snapping her gum.

"Dead ram." I'm suddenly self-conscious of the blood and plunge my hands into my pockets. The lamb sees her moment and bolts.

"Any signs of disease?"

"No," I say.

I heave the ram out of the sealed dolav bin by one leg, and he rolls onto the concrete. The stench of seaweed punctures the air. In the time it takes me to shuffle a butcher's bag around his body and seal it up, I could say something. I could ask Harper if she's following the war in Bosnia. I could think of a joke or tell her our sheep are drowning themselves. Leonela, I could ask if she saw your photo in the paper, tell her you're coming here. I could even tell her to keep an eye on the beach on her side of the headland in case you drift too far around the coast. Instead she breaks the silence by telling me I should scrub the blood off the yard before it dries, that if it's left too long it can only be removed with Coca Cola.

"Trust me, I know," she says.

Harper hoists the ram in the bag onto the back seat.

"You should bring one of the dogs by," I say. "I like dogs."

"They're not dogs, they're hunting hounds. And they're not pets. Bye, Ruby."

Her jeep roars out of the yard. The seawater outline of the ram's corpse dries on the concrete. My arms have swollen from the effort of getting the ram out of the bin. A map of purple veins begins to show itself. The nurse told me to ice them when they swell, but we don't have a freezer.

Leonela – when you're here the sheep won't die as much, and when they do we can lift them together, and the weight of them won't be as bad, won't last as long or hurt so much. We will seal the dolav bin and walk arm in arm back to the house. You'll pull up cow parsley which is a weed but you think is pretty, to put in Mother's vase on the table. You'll whistle loudly and out of tune while I bake loaf after loaf of bread until the kitchen is sweltering. We'll laugh in languages we don't understand and keep each other alive.

Oil and Vinegar

The Christian boarding school gave one free place a year to a girl from a low-income family. The vicar from our Church talked to Pa. Mrs T from the shop filled out all the forms. She told the school about Mother. Nobody asked me if I wanted to go. Pa dropped me off himself and ruffled my hair the way fathers usually reserve for their sons. He told me not to say anything silly, which was code for: don't say Mother might come back one day.

On my first night of boarding, a girl called Ariel claimed the bunk above mine and unpacked a Pink Jubilee Barbie doll. The other girls followed, pulling lifelike plastic babies from their suitcases. The dolls had eyelids that clattered open and closed, and they even drank water and pissed themselves, going through an endless cycle of tiny dresses that girls traded with each other. I watched them touch plastic spoons to their dolls' lips and thought of the way Pa forced drench nozzles far down the throats of his lambs to worm them.

I didn't have a doll, so I dragged a broken Resusci-Anne CPR dummy from the Home Economics classroom up two flights of stairs into our dormitory.

The torso was the same weight as if she were a real woman. I used a marker pen to draw eyes and eyelashes over her closed eyelids, and resuscitated her enthusiastically. Air whistled out of the rip in her chest as I breathed through her mouth. Ariel declared her 'creepy' and made me keep her under the bed. The hole in her chest got gradually bigger as I used her hollow torso to hide things from the other girls.

We didn't eat Cornish food at school because none of the other girls were Cornish. I soon forgot the richness of pilchards and shortcrust, growing used to drifting mutely behind the other girls into the kitchen late at night where they would roll up hunks of ciabatta and drag them through dishes of olive oil and balsamic vinegar that they brought back from summer holidays in Italy. They would sit cross-legged on the sideboards, tear pages out of their scripture books to make diamond-shaped paper fortune tellers which Ariel had dubbed *paku-pakus*, pincering them back and forth with their thumbs and forefingers in the four chambers like a heart, the paper walls turning like a maze to land on: *What kind of house do you live in? In which country did you spend the summer?* The balsamic vinegar left dark smudges on everything they touched, even staining the wood of the sideboards with their fingerprints.

The vinegar found its way into my skin. Into my hair, my uniform, the trace of it enduring multiple washes. Once the other girls had left for their endless milk-runs between the Mediterranean and the Caribbean and I had gone home, dragging Resusci-Anne with me, I would struggle to stomach the pilchard heads poking out of pastry in the stargazy pie that had to last us a week. I left vinegar shadows on everything I touched: I marked the trapdoor, the paddock gates, left traces of bitterness on the air that mixed with the stale cider-and-mould smell of the farmhouse. Vinegar handprints darkened Resusci-Anne's head where I hauled her about. Pa complained that something was different. Sheep would taste the acid of it in the maps of my palms and crowd me, hungry for more. I paraded Resusci-Anne back and forth to school with me, barely able to lift her but unable to leave her behind, as if practicing for a future of carrying a weight that was too heavy for me to carry alone – but there would be no choice – I would have to know how to carry it.

Milk and Money

Warblers' song finds its way through the mist in the air, bringing with it the taste of a coming storm. I wake early to check the newspaper, scanning to see if Bosnian refugees have arrived in Britain yet, but there is nothing.

When I shuffle into the yard a little before sunrise, I find a ewe on her side by the door as if waiting for help, waves rippling through her flanks. She doesn't lift her face as I kneel down: each laboured lungful of air drains the last of her energy.

Leonela - let me show you what needs to be done. Twist a hand into the ewe, find a dead lamb wedged in front of a live one. Drag the dead one out by one foot with the next contraction, feel its bones tick as you twist it out in a tangle. Throw it through the back door of the house so the ewe won't be distracted by it. Find the live lamb wedged by its shoulders. Ease one foot out to reduce the width of its chest. Use Vaseline and some cord from the lambing crate to get a noose behind its ears. Push a thumb into its mouth to check that it's swallowing, still alive, wait for the ripple of a contraction through the ewe's sides like a growing ocean swell. Now corkscrew the lamb with one hand.

There will be a final grunt from the ewe and out it floods. Hoist it up by its hind legs, beat it on the back until its face splits with a first cry, then place it under the ewe's nose. While she pants and clears away the strings of membrane, twist one of her teats to unblock it, then take off whatever you're wearing to dry the lamb; they grow cold in under a minute.

When you deliver your first lambs you'll want to name them, want to show me their first steps and point out evidence that they love or even like you. When I was young, I named every lamb that was born.

Snufkin. Snorkmaiden. Sniff. Sorry-oo.

Now every girl sheep is *Milk*, every boy sheep *Money*. All named: *Please Live.* There's nothing gentle in birth or any of the moments after.

In my pocket I find the tube of citrus sharp Polos that Mrs T let me pick out from her village shop yesterday, which reminds me that it's my birthday today. Sixteen. I use a thumbnail to push a Polo from the tube and feed it to the ewe. She leaves a string of slime along my sleeve. The lamb lifts a quivering snout, still blind, turning his head back and forth between the bleat of his mother and the distant crash of the ocean.

Pa appears in the doorway in a pair of shrunken long-johns, his eyes retaining the wet redness of last night's drinking. I'd forgotten about the dead lamb I'd tossed in through the door before the second one was born.

"Ruby," he says, holding up its liquid-boned corpse in the remaining fingers of his right hand.

"You *did* get me a birthday present," I say.

Leonela, when you arrive, long after I've hauled you in with the tide, I'll teach you how to be a sheep midwife. Your hands will be small, perfect. You'll be ready with the wide-necked jar of iodine and scissors. I'll teach you with my hand over yours, speaking only in touches. I'll make you an origami paku-paku with questions written on it and slowly, your history will come out.

There must be a Bosnian word for this kind of waiting. There must be a word for the reflection of the moon on the sea that paints a road to the horizon, for how, instead of sleeping, I gaze out of the attic skylight at the moon-road and expect to see you there, sandals in one hand and skirt bunched up in the other. You're looking for the house. You're looking for me. You and I were not stormbred like this, not born for drowning or hunger. Like warblers who scratch on the ground and find it frozen, who go to the window for oats and find it closed, we'll follow some immense and unbreakable compass we were both born with and end up together, our insistent bird-hearts blinking together on that rain-ravaged beach.

Operation Irma

I'm in Mrs T's shop watching her portable telly while I wait for her to take me to my hospital appointment. Harper comes in while I'm sitting on the collapsible steps eating out-of-date fudge that Mrs T pretends she can't sell. She stands in the doorway for a moment as if adjusting to the dimly lit shop, swaying slightly. I imagine how I look perched on the steps eating sweets and my cheeks warm. When she leans over me for a litre of Frosty Jack's, the smell of cider jets from her throat. Her face has an oily sheen to it and makeup clumps into the creases around her eyes. There are large gold hoops in her ears. I imagine the hoops on you, half-hidden in your rainfall of black hair. I imagine giving them to you, brushing your hair aside to put them in your ears for you.

I offer Harper a piece of fudge, which she takes but doesn't eat.

"I like your earrings" I say.

"You can have them," she replies, and unhooks them, tossing them to me before I can say anything. I hide them in my lap, embarrassed, not wanting to hold them with sticky hands.

"Did you see that someone jumped from Dodman's Point?" she asks. "At the weekend."

"Why?" I ask obediently. I want to say that if she doesn't want the fudge, I'll have it back.

"Gambling addiction. Up to his eyeballs in debt. His wife was in the paper," Mrs T says from behind the counter.

Harper lolls her head back and rolls her eyes at this. Mrs T glares at her as she pays for the cider with a tenner. The shop is silent as she sulks out without saying goodbye, and after the door closes Mrs T says she's all trouble. "I wouldn't serve her, you know," she defends herself, "but I can't afford to upset her Ma."

Footage from a Bosnian hospital comes on the telly: a little girl called Irma with blonde hair in a hospital bed, torso bound in bandages. Her head bends back and her eyes fix on something high above her, the angle of her neck like a new lamb struggling to breathe. Her fingernails are still flecked with pink nail polish that I imagine her mother, now dead, had painted for her. A plastic dolly with yellow hair lies on the pillow beside her, and there's bouquet of blood spots on the sheet, a single petal on her upper lip. Her bluebell eyes snap open for a moment, then flutter closed again, doll-like.

The news cuts to the surgeon who is saying that Irma has forty-eight hours to live if she is not evacuated on a medical plane. She was injured by a mortar shell while she visited a market with her Mother in Sarajevo. The surgeon says the angle of Irma's spine and neck is an indicator of brain damage setting in. It cuts from the surgeon to John Major, who is saying he is sending the RAF to bring her here, along with twenty other children who are to be medically evacuated to British hospitals for treatment. I think back to the pictures in the paper of the injured across Bosnia, the growing figures that have been in the headlines. Twenty doesn't sound like a lot. A sweeping shot shows the children being prepared by British soldiers, wrapped in orange blankets with IVs still attached. The same surgeon is saying that they have nothing at the hospital: that they wash and reuse bandages, that they have no cleaning solution and are treating wounds with water. No electricity. Surgery by torch light.

Leonela. I don't look for you amongst the children. You won't be there. Not blonde enough. Too old. Overlooked for the injuries you lack. Too lovely as you endure the ones you have. I'll use one fold of paper in the paku-paku to ask you where it hurts, and you will be able to tell me: *everywhere, everywhere.*

Aniseed Balls

Ariel had taken to eating aniseed balls because she liked the smell of them, so when I walked into our dorm, I was hit with the pepper-liquorice pinch of them. We were thirteen so we were allowed into town after school. Ariel put her head inside each dorm without knocking, rounding up a group of girls to go to Jitterbugs, and they went together in berets and metallic leggings, tight together like a flock.

After they left, I asked our dormitory mentor Sister Shiloh for oats and loaf ends. Ariel didn't share her aniseed balls with me so I swiped a packet of them from her trunk. I spent the afternoon being 'Aurelia'. I walked along the outskirts of town to the river as an Aurelia might walk – Aurelia had no interest in drinking coke floats – but the river had dried to mud. I looked for the warblers, imagining Aurelia might want to sketch them or put them in a poem, but only herring gulls stamped up and down the riverbed where they pulled worms out of mud that smelled of sewage. Unlike the autumn-grey of the warblers, the gulls had bodies like snowdrifts, their beaks sunshine-yellow. I beckoned them to me, crouching down and chirruping, holding oats out in my hand and dropping the bread at my feet.

The gulls didn't tip their heads at me shyly. They didn't rock on bent-pin legs or bounce closer across the mud. They rushed at me, their open beaks turning to bottomless caverns. They arched their wings and beat the air into a storm. When they screamed, man-words climbed their throats. The Aurelia I had imagined would have stood her ground, but I could not be Aurelia as I fell backwards, dropping the oats. The gulls' faces became sour whirlpools as they swallowed whole bread slices and turned on each other, ripped into each other for more.

I imagined Ariel, sitting on a stool at a bar across town, ignoring her coke float in its tall glass, her favourite songs lined up on the jukebox. Another girl would be braiding her hair for her while she held an elaborate paku-paku on her thumbs and forefingers. Other girls would choose numbers and colours for Ariel to lift the paper corners and instruct them: Tell a secret you've never told anyone. *Tell a joke with sex in it. Tell a secret about a girl at this table. Tell a secret about a girl who's not here.*

One herring gull made a grab for my bag and I threw it high into the air. The sky was alive with noise and snow. They ripped open the aniseed balls. As they snatched the packet from each other there was the familiar smell of it on the air, so strong I almost knew the taste. They brought the weather alive, as though snow that once muffled the fields and blocked out the sun had learned to sing and turn to straws of light that needled the earth around me.

On the walk back to school it was already growing dark and any far-off fire of stars was pushed away further by streetlamps. Stiff from the cold and with mud on the back of my school skirt, I didn't stop to press my face to the window of Jitterbugs. Aurelia would have walked inside and sat coolly alone with a book. Aurelia had tried aniseed and did not care for it. I was not Aurelia. I didn't listen to the music on the jukebox. The inside of the small café was somehow a larger world. I was on the outside looking into it, pressed up against it, looking for a way in, but there was more than glass between us.

Pigs in Wigs

Pa bought our Beltex sheep after he saw them at the Royal Cornwall Show where they were presented ass-first to show off the way their over-bred rumps flowed over delicate bones. Half Belgian and half Dutch, they'd been imported, so Pa had to go to Wigan to buy a mob. He drove them the seven hours home, and when he lowered the ramp in the yard one of the rams was dead from heatstroke. Pa waved a hand dismissively and said we would make the loss back in no time, that he had seen yearlings go for a hundred and fifty a piece. He slapped the closest ewe on the backside and she strutted down the ramp, staring me down with eyes the colour of the seabed, eyes fixed in the front of her head like a hawk. She had the dumb, bulging jaw of a bare-knuckle boxer. I inched away.

They barely looked like sheep. *Pigs in wigs,* Pa called them. You couldn't say he loved them, but he showed the kind of pride in them that people usually reserve for their children. He'd leave the house before dawn after pouring undrunk dregs of juice back into the carton, eating whole apples, core and stem, along with the plug of butterfat from the top of the bottle of sheep's milk. Long after sunset I'd be standing on a stool to reach the sink, using a fork to de-scale pilchards for stargazy pie, and I'd hear Pa's tools outside as he reinforced fencing. The tell-tale beam of his head torch would occasionally sweep through the kitchen window, lighting up the scales in the sink. I'd lean out of the skylight at night and see him turning over sheep one by one as though dismantling the moon itself, checking it for ailments.

Leonela - I'm trying to recall a memory of Pa without sheep around him, and it's true that he once bought me an Easter Egg: I smashed it open to eat the Smarties inside, and he was washing dishes and singing *Shine, Jesus, Shine*. When he got to the chorus, he couldn't remember it and paused theatrically with a plate hoisted high, suds poised along its rim, and then launched into the chorus of *Come on Eileen*. I laughed as he tossed dishes onto the rack, creating snowdrifts of bubbles, then he took my hand, still holding my Smarties, to go to the paddocks. He must have known the rest of *Shine, Jesus, Shine*. We sang it every week in church. But it's long and repetitive and he didn't want to finish it. He wanted to show me how to prod a finger, still purple with food colouring, into the mouths of the ewes to check for Orf Virus, or how to lift their tails to check for flystrike.

Then, two years ago, the wind blew a Chinese lantern onto the headland and it burned down the barn. The sheep survived, but Pa lost four fingers getting them out. The insurance company claimed that Pa had built the barn from a cheap and flammable material, and wouldn't pay out. I came home from school at Christmas to find him bare-chested and asleep on the sofa at three in the afternoon. I stood with my sleeve over my mouth as I approached his Bible table that was cluttered with Skreach bottles. The flowers had been left to dry and drop onto the table, as if each day had shed its own skin. The doily that I had made was stained brown by dead petals. The candles were burned down to stubs, wax flooded over the table and glued the crucifixes. The Bible was closed.

And it's true the lambs are born with muscle. I wrestle with the ewes during lambing season as they struggle to birth babies with squashed, lumpy skulls and bodies like pitbulls. Sometimes when I place the newborns under the snouts of the ewes, they snort and turn away as if they don't recognise what it is that they've birthed. Sometimes they sit on their own lambs in the night or knock them into water troughs. The ones that survive struggle under the weight of muscles that tumefy faster than their bones can grow. By six months old, panting as the bulge of their brawn weighs on their lungs, they are ready for slaughter.

Cornish hedges are not enough to keep Beltexes contained. The sheep shove their way through them, clamber over post and rail fencing with ease. Push through electric tape and pig wire unharmed, drag barbed wire off the posts in their fleeces. They've learned not to escape during the day. I come down to the beach with the first light and there's usually one struggling out at sea like a fleck of flotsam, paddling against the current. Sometimes there's one already dead and washed up onto the stones. Bloated, legs at terrible angles in the cold air. I've saved a couple. Swum out, dragged them in by their necks. Hauled them back to the paddock where the sea tumbles in their lungs. Their deaths by drowning are drawn out over the next week.

Since the fire, the farm has barely looked like a farm, barely seemed like somewhere living things could thrive. It's no more than a lightning strike on a cliff edge. Pa wakes in the night because he's had asthma since the fire, as well as bouts of pneumonia, so I move to the attic to sleep in the dinghy. No bed to make in the mornings. No mark of having slept at all, no evidence of dreaming.

Leonela, I've nearly finished making your paku-paku. Each new fold of paper asks you about the sea, about loneliness.

Sing me songs 'til the end.
What's the coldest you've been and have you seen
death?
What are girls made of?
I dare you to drink this cider.
I dare you to never drink again.

Pink Jubilee Barbie Doll

Far from the farmhouse, perched in the scrubbed white and bleach-wet floors of the hospital examination room, I'm aware of the dirt on my hands and the sheep drool on my jumper, the blood flecks that have blackened over time. Aware, too, of the cloying cider-smell lingering in my hair. The cleanness here stings my nostrils. I ask the nurse if any of the children from Bosnia have come. He pinches up and down my forearm where skin stretches across ploughed bone.

"Squeeze my hand, Ruby. Can't you squeeze any harder? What children?"

"My ... Leonela is coming." Saying *friend* or *girlfriend* doesn't sound right. "But she has to come by dinghy."

"You need another x-ray. You should have come sooner." He flicks through a file. "It says here I need to sign something for a lawsuit? How are you finding the Tramadol?"

"I dream a lot."

I'm halfway out the exam room when he adds: "You should make a separate appointment if you want to talk about your face," and clicks the door closed.

I've only seen my face reflected in the water trough and the skylight glass for the last four months. Pa has a shaving mirror but it's three inches across and I haven't noticed anything different. I tell Mrs T that I need the loo, then use the disabled one so she can't check on me.

I grip the sink with both hands as I lean into my reflection. It's as though there's a pucker in the mirror. The orb of bone around my right eye socket has changed shape: the cheekbone droops about a millimetre. It leaves the right eyeball too exposed, the red wetness inside the eyelid just visible. Skin slackens on the side of my face, sagging from the jawbone. The right corner of my mouth sulks. All in the tiniest amounts. All in miniscule, devastating margins. I'm reminded, obscenely, of the mask for the school play that was forgotten and left to melt in the heat of a stage light.

I think, too, of my photograph of you that keeps one side of your face frozen forever behind your hand, and I cover the right side of my face with my left hand to see how it looks. I think, too, of Ariel, who would come through the window in the cold, dead hours and switch on our shared bed lamp. I'd silently roll over to hang my head from the bunk, watch as she used a handkerchief dipped in olive oil to slick the tear-streaked makeup from her face and then apply it all again, until she looked like a doll that had never been played with. A mint condition Pink Jubilee Barbie, still in her box.

The Refugee Council chose your photo for their fundraising campaign, your half-face as the face of Bosnian suffering, made *pretty* a burden, a weight for you to carry and never put down. I didn't know what the nurse meant by "talk about my face", but I would no longer think about masking the dirty freckles sown across the bridge of my nose, or wonder if I could grow the width of my bird chest. *Pretty* was a door slammed closed.

Mrs T beams at me when I emerge, tossing a copy of *Ideal Home* back onto the waiting room table. Since I could remember, she had always delivered a tree to our house on Christmas Eve, saying it was a leftover at the shop. She acted like we were doing her a favour, taking it off her hands. She pretended not to see me stealing toilet paper and soap from her staff loo. She had a sixth sense, and recognised my hunger.

You will be in this hospital, Leonela, sometime soon. Your clothes will be a map of the world's dust, your hair will smell of war and the city. The same nurse will say you should have come sooner. When we walk out of here, we'll leave footprints on the mopped floor. There'll be flaking blood, bone that shifts like tectonic plate. Puddles of seawater will follow. Enough of the ocean to drown in. I've added more questions to your paku-paku:

What's the prettiest thing you've seen?
What's the hungriest?
If not pretty, then what else?

Passing the Paku-Paku

I'm de-fleaing myself using mayonnaise and garlic, so I still have a plastic bag over my head when I walk around Dodman's Point on the splinter of headland that keeps Vault Beach in shadow, then down to the shore to check for straying sheep. Imagine my excitement when I see the dinghy dragged onto the sand at low tide. Imagine how I run to flip it over, then spin around madly looking for you or your footprints to see where you might have staggered, delirious from dehydration.

I even say *Leonela* out loud, only to see the figures of three girls far down the beach, at the nudist end, passing a joint back and forth and rummaging for firewood at the base of the cliffs. I spit in the sand. The girls have left navy blue jumpers in the dinghy and they're now in the sand where I've flipped it over. I pick one up: a school hockey team jumper, smelling of weed and the type of perfume Ariel wore before disappearing at night. I throw two jumpers in the dinghy and put on the third, the cuffs past my fingertips, then plant a foot on the dinghy and press, testing it. It's better than the one at home. I push it into the water and belly flop into it, using a foot to push off the seabed until I'm carried away in the current. I kneel up to look back at the shore. The three girls are knee-deep in the water and waving wildly at me. Probably shouting, the black spots of their mouths visible as the wind picks up and whips their voices up the cliffs.

I wash up on the sand near the farmhouse and lie under the jumpers, enjoying how they smell neither of cider or mould, when the front end of the dinghy sinks and I look up to see Harper leaning over me, her hands on either side of my face. She breathes the warm smell of Frosty Jack's over my face, which mixes with the weed smell from the jumpers and the sweat from the sea. Her eyeliner has smudged so that her eyes bloom across her face. Her skin has a grey pallor to it, with yellowish circles under her eyes. She looks as though she's been in the sea, wet underwear darkening its outline through her clothes. I sit up to face her.

"Ruby," she says. "Your Pa rang and said you had a dead lamb for me. Why is there a plastic bag on your head?"

I forgot about the mayonnaise and garlic in my hair.

"Oh yeah. Stillborn."

"And why do you have three of the same jumper?"

"Living for excess. Want one?"

"No. Can we just go and get the lamb?"

I don't want to walk up the coast path with her. In all the ways that Ariel was exquisite and frightening when she came back to the dorm drunk, Harper seems sluggish and humourless, not to mention a little sick. I also know that she's too drunk to drive her jeep home and I should make her stay and sober up. I even indulge a brief fantasy of confiscating her keys, hiding them inside Resusci-Anne. But I don't want her to stay. I want to lie in the dinghy under the bruised sky and in the layers of dead seaweed and wait with a dry jumper, ready for you.

Leonela – in real life you'll be cherry black and apple flesh white and together we'll be nothing charming or lovely. We'll lie in the dinghy upstairs, our combined weight pressing the air from it, and slough our layers and skins as well, then peel back the old injuries, the snapped kindling of our bones, sea-salt sores and all the nights of sleep for dinner, all the mornings of waking to the sound of rats, lungs hacking up spores. We'll pass a paku-paku back and forth all night, until the warmth of our fingers curls its paper corners and renders it useless. When we've shed it all, asked all the questions and dawn brings a deluge of old light to the attic, we'll be cleaner, and the deflated dinghy will take us somewhere.

Sweet Česnica Christmas Bread

It took years for Pa to tell me that Mother's name was Milena, that he shortened it to Millie. He didn't tell me her surname or keep photos or give me anything of hers, but when I moved into the attic, I found her mink coat that Pa had probably intended to sell, as well as something folded and hand-written. There was a flicker of excitement as I thought it might be a letter left for me, but it was just a hand-written recipe for Sweet Christmas Bread.

Pa thinks that because he didn't keep photos that I don't know what Mother looked like, but I have a newborn memory of her sitting across the kitchen and smoking by the window that has not been opened. Knees drawn up, tiny sheep-midwife hands. Her body is as neatly packaged and self-contained as a warbler's egg. She is as far away from me as possible. She looks too small to be a mother, and maybe she was, labouring for two days in the back seat of the jeep that never started, no ambulance on the way because the phone had been cut off again.

Even when drunk, Pa has only said that Mother is *gone up North*, but to Pa that means anywhere across the Tamar, so when I picture where she might be now I often imagine her in a town square, drinking coffee under a statue, but because she looks too much like me in my imagination I can't help thinking of the waiter who is staring at her, angry because she has done something like eaten all of the sugar cubes out of the bowl, and he thinks she is weird for something she's wearing or the way she is sitting, and nobody is greeting her or sitting near her.

I made her bread recipe for Christmas the year of the barn fire, using butter from the school kitchen that Sister Shiloh sent me home with, saying it would go bad over the holidays. Pa gave me a five pence piece to put inside the baking tin on the condition that he have it back afterwards. The recipe said to use extra dough to make religious decoration on the top of the loaf, so I spent a full morning crafting Jesus's face, rolling each strand of hair between my palms. The recipe didn't specify to use dough without yeast for this part, so Jesus came out of the oven bloated beyond recognition. Pa got the five pence piece in his slice.

"It's lucky!" I cried. "What do you wish for?" I wasn't sure if it came with a wish but offered one anyway.

"Fer Chrissake, Ruby, I nearly broke my jaw," he said. "My gar, did you even wash this?" He held the coin up to inspect it and then threw his slice in the bin.

At school in January, I told Ariel the story about the swollen Jesus face, how he looked as though he had fallen into a wasp's nest, a tentative experiment to see if Ariel would laugh.

"Was your mum Serbian?" she asked. "Sweet Christmas Bread is a Serbian recipe. Our au pair used to make it, it's called Česnica Bread. What was your mum's name?"

"Millie. Milena."

"Sounds pretty fucking Serbian to me."

Česnica. From the word cest, meaning *to share.* I'd never seen Pa throw away food before. I spent Christmas Day sitting with the baking dish in my lap, eating my way through the entire loaf, using my fingernails to dig out the burnt dough that was glued into the corners, until there was nothing left and I was stretched out, beached in my chair in the sugar-choked kitchen. As the sun went down I couldn't even move to fill the oil lamps, so sat alone in coarse darkness, scraping at traces of sugar and butter. What else was there room for after that?

The Blood of the Bird

By the time I come in from morning feeds Pa is already onto the cider, washed up on the sofa with his shirt hanging open, reading the sports section of the paper while the cover that bears Irma's photo lies discarded on the floor. I turn around and go back outside, taking the shotgun from the porch to see if Pa notices. I lie on my back in the paddock in the warm air that hums beneath the bruised sky, waiting for a fox to be tempted into view by the new lamb with the black face, or threads of afterbirth still cobwebbing between the hindlegs of the ewe. An hour goes by before I see a brush of amber in the hedge. I fire before it can get away.

The recoil from the shotgun punches me hard in the shoulder and heat sprints into both forearms. The pheasant had been resting in the hedge and upon being shot, pirouettes like a ballerina with ribbons of blood leaping from its side, then scrambles a few feet in the grass. I pick it up and turn it over in my hands. Its beak twitches open and its eyes spin before coming to rest. The heavy globe of its head rolls in my palm, turning from blue to green and back to blue, like the sea when a storm is building.

The pheasants belong to Harper's family, reserved for European shooting parties who stay in the castle on the opposite coast and eat game for three meals a day. I crouch in the grass with my ears singing from the gunshot, waiting to see if Pa is coming, before forcing the pheasant under my sweater. Blood dots my boots and the tail plumage splays from under my collar as if I'm trying to surprise someone with an oversized bouquet.

My arms are too weak from the shotgun recoil to climb the gate so I have to slide under it, blood like an oil slick under my jumper. I trip over pebbles until I'm knee deep in the sea. A wave barrels into me like a ram. Ripping the bird from under my sweater, I throw it high into the air. A final pinwheel of blood spins from its falling body and air whistles from its lungs in a small 'oh' of surprise as it turns over in the sky. The last ebb of it strings on the water. I let the waves continue to batter me, staggering each time. Copper feathers appear and disappear again with each swell. Sister Shiloh would treat any ailment with salt water. She'd soak a green paper towel and clap it, stinging hard, over our grazed elbows and cut knees.

Back home, I stuff my boots with newspaper and hide them in the attic instead of in front of the fire. My arms have swollen so much I've lost the feeling in my thumbs, so I struggle to break the shotgun and replace the cartridge, fretting over the precise position I had found it in. I'm in the attic and hear Pa rise from his torpor after dark while I'm using an old nail to gouge dried blood from under my fingernails. I kick through the clothes on the floor. Pheasant blood has soaked through everything and spattered across the floorboards. Although it barely produced more blood than a difficult lambing, the jumper I was wearing is heavy with it. Resusci-Anne lies at the foot of the dinghy, the hinge of her neck extended so her head is pushed back. A single spot of red shines on her upper lip. I drop to my knees, scrubbing at the stain with my thumb and finally sucking on it to try and clean it away. Strangely delicious. Still it remains on her drowned, over-kissed mouth. Her inked-on eyes stare me down and there is a whisper of Ariel's perfume still about her. There is nothing left inside her torso except your paku-paku that asks questions about violence as if I've never seen violence, and your photo from the paper, tightly folded to hide your face away from all of this.

The Warbler's Prison

While Ariel was away for the night, I slept in her bed next to her Pink Jubilee Barbie, rubbing one of her slippery braids against my cheek and flicking through Ariel's shoebox of photos. There was a photo of Ariel posing in a short dress at a funfair, a likely favourite as it was the only photo to be put in a clip frame. I took it and hid it inside Resusci-Anne under the bed.

Ariel was pale and mute when she returned from the hospital. She twisted and sweated on the bunk above me, and woke in the night to shuffle to the bathroom clutching thick sanitary towels. I offered her the lower bunk, but she ignored me. I thought of the ewes that bellowed in the night, the particular sound when I knew I would reach the pasture to find their newborns strewn about by foxes, how they moaned for days afterwards, beached and inconsolable on their sides. Nearing adulthood, I'm rendered more startled and bird-like than ever. Pa and Mrs T thought I needed Mother when I was young and less so now, but it was at times like this that I scrutinised the memory of Mother and tried to draw her away from the window, so I could take the cigarette from her and ask *what do I do here?*

When Ariel failed to move from our bunk for a third day, I whistled a warbler down to the window and brought it into the dormitory on a forefinger. It bounced off the walls for a moment before settling, ruffled and self-conscious on a bed post. Ariel eased herself upright in bed as she tried to draw it onto her duvet with pieces of crystallised apricot. She was so enamoured by the bird that when it was time to get dressed up to decorate the Christmas tree in the library, she lent me a cheongsam dress that her father had brought her from Hong Kong that she said had never fitted her. I spent the evening in bare feet and shuffling with my knees tied together by cool silk, smelling of Ariel's perfume, the other girls asking me with almost empirical enquiry how I became so thin.

If Ariel hadn't grown out of paku-pakus, she might have made one for me. She kept the warbler in the room, aggressively banning anyone from turning on the ceiling fan, and even cleaned its crap off the floor. Its nervous chittering woke us before dawn each day. I delayed telling her that it would die if it stayed inside.

"It's like it already knew you, the way it came to the window," Ariel said to me as she ran the back of a finger down the warbler's breast feathers.

I wanted to say yes, we both grew up together in the cold, and that's how you have to whistle a warbler, as if your whole body is cold and always has been, as if your lips are cold and blowing out cold air, as if by some miracle you have found yourself less cold and now you're calling out to say *come, it's not quite so cold here.* The electric lights had paled its pale feathers paler. It had stopped singing altogether. It waited patiently to be returned to the freedom of hunger and cold, the freedom to do the difficult things it was born to do.

The Dolly Lamb

Pa has disappeared and I'm in the attic, slick with sweat and pinned to the dinghy as if lost in a storm. The black-faced lamb that was born on my birthday sleeps beside me, sometimes wobbling to his feet with a creak of plastic only to flop onto his side again. My right arm, which had held the shotgun, burns and grows hills of bone in the wrong places. Newspapers are spread out on the floor where I had looked for hints of your location in the war reports, but Operation Irma is over and the news has forgotten Bosnia. *Jurassic Park* expects to make forty million in its first weekend. Uranus passes Neptune. President Clinton announces an outbreak of Hantavirus in four states, which comes from deer mice that hide in people's homes. It has already killed a dozen people. A dozen people doesn't sound like much anymore.

The black-faced lamb lost an eye to crows. His empty eye socket puckers and twitches as he blinks. He mews gently and paddles his legs as if he, too, endures the storm. I found him early in the morning with his legs peddling as his mother stood twenty feet away, exhausted as a rabbit in a trap. Her entire udder was beyond help: cold and black as the sea.

Drifting in and out of sleep, infection moving like smashed glass under my skin, I dream that you and I are contaminated by the lamb, that he infects us like deer mice. We wake with saltwater in our lungs and the ocean pulling us to it. I have one hand on the door frame and the other wrapped around your hair as I try to stop you from going. My right arm breaks all over again as I beg you to stay. I wake myself calling *Leonela* out loud, and upon waking I plug the lamb's eye socket with fresh cotton balls soaked in leucillin, and shove a bottle teat in his mouth, forcing colostrum into him. He pants and remains on his side, swims some more.

I'm hauled from semi-consciousness by the sound of Harper's jeep on the yard, and I remember the pheasant that will be washed up on a beach somewhere with the betrayal of shrapnel in its side. I stumble down the ladder and fall into the kitchen. Harper is in the porch next to the shotgun, her nose against the glass. The grey pallor of her face has turned white, almost translucent. She's thinner, nearly as small as Ariel. Trapped, I open the door. Her smile falters as she sees me and I realise I'm not dressed.

"Did Pa call you?" I ask casually. "There's a ewe but she's got sepsis from mastitis. Probably not suitable for the hounds. You can take her if you want though." If I can shoot the ewe now then nobody will know when the shotgun was last used.

"No, I just remembered you said you wanted to see a hound. I brought a puppy. Look." She turns to the jeep where a dog hangs from the window, liquid-limbed and shining in the mid-afternoon sun, stretching its snout towards us. Hounds can smell foxes hiding forty feet underground. They would easily pick up the scent of pheasant blood spilled in a hedge, trailed along a paddock and under a gate. I can't even invite her inside where the hound will smell the blood in the attic, the traces of down stuck in the wool of my jumper, the smell of it on Resusci-Anne.

"Maybe we could go see your new lamb?" she continues. "Or we can go swimming. I've never even seen the lambs. When they're alive, I mean."

Drops of sweat hop unevenly down my temple and bead along my jaw. I imagine the hound sprinting confidently across the paddock, scattering sheep, reappearing with copper feathers fanning triumphantly from its jaw.

"The lamb is dying," I say. "It's upstairs."

"What about the rest of them?"

I shrug. We stare at each other through the heat of the silence.

"Jesus Christ," Harper mutters to herself, shaking her head. It sounds awful, the way she says it, worse than if she had sworn at me. Her cheeks scarlet, she tosses her keys in her hand and walks back to the jeep without another word. As she leaves, I notice she's wearing box-white shoes instead of mucker boots. She slams the door so hard the hound whimpers. As her jeep peels out of the yard, the hound turns his face to look at me and I quickly slam the front door.

When I open the trapdoor, the attic is warm and the fetid air carries the smell of death. The lamb lies still and with his head peeled back in the bottom of the dinghy. He looks like a doll: sewn-on snout, buttoned-up eyes and capable of a drawstring cry. He looks as though he could be taken to boarding school, cuddled and cried into, a spare blazer button sewn over his empty eye socket, named Bella Izza or Annie-Panny, stitched and smoothed by some girl who had got pregnant or hooked on Prozac or was starving herself half to death. But just as I sit on the edge of the dinghy and lend him the easy immortality of the dollmaker's needle, he takes a sputtering breath as if inhaling through water, and his legs flounder again. He stretches his nose out to catch the scent of the wretched sea that barrels in through the open trapdoor, and resumes his tireless drowning.

The Release of Barabbas

It was during a Saturday scripture class that we were required to write, from memory, the biblical account of the release of Barabbas. According to the Gospel of Luke, he was the riot leader who Pontius Pilate freed at the Passover Feast where it was tradition to exonerate one prisoner, and the story went that Jesus was overlooked and remained in jail awaiting execution. The week before it had been Ariel's turn to choose an extract and she picked something from the Book of Leviticus so that she could glare meaningfully at the text and then bug her eyes out at me as Sister Shiloh read the part about killing gay people. Pa favoured the Gospel of Luke when I was young because it was mostly about poor people and farmers, so I was first to finish my summary and be excused to breakfast.

On Monday, Sister Shiloh told me I was summoned to the headteacher, and when I entered her office, she had my scripture book in her hand, tossing it onto her desk as if it were unsanitary. She asked if I had something to say for myself and my recent essay. I reiterated that I thought the anecdote of the release of Barabbas seemed farfetched, saying I couldn't imagine Pontius Pilate, backed by the Roman army, getting peer pressured by a crowd at a party into releasing a murderer who had rioted against the Empire.

"Believe it or not Ruby, you're not the first student who thinks deconstructing the Gospel makes you look smart," she said. She reminded me that, as per my bursary, it was an expectation that Pa and I were God-fearing.

There were other expectations too, like pretending that Mother and Pa were married and that Mother was dead, but she didn't mention those. I wondered what the expectations were of Ariel, who sold whiskey miniatures and Ritalin out of our dorm, who would return through our window late at night, weeping after more sex with the wrong boys, and would often shake one or more of us awake to accuse us of stealing from her.

Looking back, it's a shame I didn't break my arms earlier. I could have folded the Tramadol tablets inside origami hearts, named them Chill Pills or Dream Pellets and made more money than the farm makes in a year.

I was reminded of this summoning to the headteacher, after which I had given a cowardly apology, when I was looking for Bosnian words to learn. After Ariel had asserted that Mother was probably Serbian, I had taken a Slavik languages book from the library, which stayed in my bedframe somewhere until Sister Shiloh sent it home with the rest of my exercise books. Today, it was in this book that I found variations of 'baraba' in different Slavik languages. *Drifter, pauper, vagabond.* And I hoped that the story from the Gospel of Luke wasn't true, because I thought that Jesus, in the unlikely event that he existed, would have been confident that the crowd at the Passover Feast would choose him to be released. When the guards pulled Barabbas from the cell and the two of them squinted against the pinhole aperture of light from the April sun through the open doorway, Jesus would have sunk back to the floor and watched Barabbas go, watched him not look back, readjusted his eyes as the cell door clanged him back into darkness.

Leonela, you will be watching as children are chosen for empty spaces in boats. Girls with injuries, boys with cash. Watching them pull down their coats where they were drying on tents and barbed wire fences, unsure of where to go, saying hasty goodbyes. Cold air moves to fill the spaces where they stood. You will still be sitting, breaking your single piece of bread into pieces in case any warblers pass over. But they, too, sense the war in the weather and travel on.

Hunger and Happiness

The sun has returned to scarcity. The sheep are at sea, the warblers have flown somewhere warmer. I am alone and disappearing under sedimentary layers of sea salt and sheep sweat. In an attempt to avoid calls from debt collectors I missed calls from Sister Shiloh, so she wrote a letter asking me to forgive. Whenever girls came back after Christmas with highlights in their hair or newly pierced ears, and with new songs from the TV as if they'd learned another new language without me, she made the effort to ask how my holiday was. She would catch me eating too much, stuffing oranges and unpeeled boiled eggs into my blazer pockets while I crammed triangles of buttered toast into my mouth and would pretend not to notice. She cried when she drove me to the hospital and she was the first grown woman I had ever seen cry. Because of all this, I wanted to forgive. But, like rolling your tongue, or whistling, or understanding jokes, forgiveness is something you must be born with.

The lamb with the black face now lives in the kitchen with a bandana wrapped around his face. Harper hasn't come around since she came with the puppy. If I call about fallen stock she doesn't pick up the phone. Grass grows long in the paddocks and the wind crimps it into waves, which the sheep wade through, bellowing to each other or standing alone in their private misery.

Beyond the exposed needle of Dodman's Point, the sea aches from recent storms. More greedy than ever, suckling the rain from the sky. I cannot pray for your safety, but I hope for it badly. With Harper ignoring my calls, I no longer retrieve the sheep from the ocean because I have nowhere to put their bodies. I can see them from the cliff top like vessels untied on the water: sometimes it looks as though they are still alive, the wrinkles of the sea carrying them like strands of stratus, and the sea smells different because of them. When one washes up on a beach along the coast, hikers must hurry to drag in what looks like a washed-up dog, until they realise it has the face of a dog but the ears of a pig and the body of something ugly. They'll cover their mouths with their sleeves, unable to get close to such a lost and stormbred creature, corpulent, unrecognisable and far from home.

At home, the black face lamb whines with surprising endurance in the house somewhere. I take a double dose of Tramadol to sleep through it. What will happen when you haul your dinghy in, only to find the shore teeming with shadows? How will we spend our days once the sheep are dead and the paddocks grow over, shrouding the splinter of our farmhouse from the world? I'll show you how to use the paku-paku, but when I try to get you to choose a number or colour, you'll stare blankly. I'll fill the vase with footlong stalks of cow parsley that will tower over the table, shedding. I'll drift around in the dinghy for days until I net a cuttlefish, which I'll drag in for you to make *crni rizot*, and you'll recoil because it's too big and still has the tentacles attached. We'll have the wrong rice and there'll be no white wine in the house. In pleading with you I'll shorten your name to a more British *Leo* and you'll scream at me, apple-flesh face turned red, whipping your monsoon of hair. The cuttlefish will slump on the kitchen table, leaking. I'll fail to fully scrub the smell of it from the dinghy and you'll move to sleep in the bathtub. I'll go to kiss you and you'll twist away. I'll put cow parsley in every mug, every glass in the house. The kitchen will come alive with flies. In my worst nightmare, you're hungry.

Leonela – I used to fantasise that if Mother returned, she'd rage at Pa for letting me be like this – but maybe it is me who she would be angry with – and it wouldn't be the fury that comes tied to love, but cold fury alone. Don't you think that, in Bosnian, the word *hunger* sounds too much like *happiness*?

Language becomes murky. Something to be rifled through, elbow-deep, something to be pillaged and squandered. You are losing your mother tongue and I am too slow to learn it. Words become a hostile ocean that thunders between us.

Silk Squares

You might wonder why I have mentioned to you only Ariel and no other girls. The truth is that they existed alongside me with a kind of mystery, as if they all spoke a language I had never learned. For a year I didn't notice that Renxiang, in the opposite bunk, had a paralysed arm: the result of an electrical accident in Shenzhen as a child. I only found out because Ariel spat this at her as an insult one night: Renxiang braided her hair, tied her laces and played hockey with such single-handed grace that I'd never noticed, and when I did, I felt ashamed of Pa. How easily he had become undone. The loss of four fingers had knocked him down in a manner from which he'd never recovered. I even found it pathetic that he'd turned his back on the church when God had been very much real to him. At home I would sometimes try to goad him into a fight, finding his fury less frightening than his stupors, saying only a moron would buy a foreign breed of sheep he had no idea how to raise, questioning if he begged Mother to stay or even asked her, but this rarely worked and usually he would gaze at me with glassy eyes, a blanket pulled up to his chin, or he would wander off to a neighbouring farm to find some other old farmer to drink with.

Renxiang would sometimes sprint to the row of payphones to talk to her father who made rushed calls on layovers between flights, and I would loiter in the booth with the broken phone to listen. He also visited unexpectedly, always in a linen suit, always leaving the meter on the taxi running. He would fold one arm around a beaming Renxiang, and he'd hand something to Sister Shiloh - turkish delight or bangles to be shared around, tiny brass board games for the library - and my cheeks would burn at the idea of Pa showing up, unshaven and in a filthy vest, something bloody and disturbing in the back of the jeep, and what could he bring other than a washed out Skreach bottle full of sheep's milk?

Renxiang's father visited on the day of the total eclipse. The other girls had made pinhole boxes without me and wouldn't share, so in spite of Sister Shiloh's warning I defiantly looked at the sky and the sun burned itself onto my retinas, refusing to be blinked away.

I was in bed with a paper towel full of ice over my eyes when Ariel fell through the window after dark, tottering across the dorm. She went to climb the ladder to her bunk with her heels still on and

I reached for her leg to get her attention without waking anyone, aiming for her calf but touching her thigh in the darkness.

"Ren's dad brought silk squares this evening," I whispered. "I saved you one."

I'd only taken one for her and not for myself, sensing that silk squares were not designed to be paired with a boiler suit speckled with sheep's blood. I held it out. She sat on the edge of my bed. Her shoulders curled over. Tears glittered on her face and she hiccupped softly.

"Ruby. Put it on me." I set down the paper towel of ice and looped the silk around her delicate throat, and she tipped her head back while I knotted it.

"How do I look?" Her knees were drawn up to her chest.

"Beautiful, you always look beautiful," I stumbled over my words, "like a doll, a Pink Jubilee Barbie doll ..."

"Pretty?" Her voice was catching.

"Yes of course. Perfect--"

And I was cut off by her wet face pressed imprecisely to mine, her hair spilling across it and her wet lashes butterflying against my sore eyes, her mouth pushed against the corner of mine. Her silk scarf moved between us like a breeze. She was as thin as a layer of ice I could fall through. And then she was asleep, and everything was different in the world. I could survive the absence of warblers. Who cared whether the last of the sheep died and whether Pa drowned himself on the sofa or followed them into the sea? Who cared for the sea? My closed eyes burned. I was happy to have faced the sun head-on.

I should have moved to her bed and left her in mine. Instead, I lay under the hot weight of her, vodka and perfume breathed softly onto my neck. Ice melted through the paper towel and soaked the pillow. I didn't move. My arms were pinned so I couldn't lift a hand to where her mouth had imprinted itself on my face. The feel of it stayed through the night, burned into my skin with the strength and rareness of an emerging midday sun.

The Girl on the Edge

Hunger had me open-eyed and sleepless so I saw it unmistakably – there was something on the horizon, something a little after midnight. Something like a beam of light swinging through the skylight and briefly illuminating the bloody floorboards, Resusci-Anne's drowned face. Hopes of a refugee rescue boat and fears of a second Chinese lantern send me running, still in my underwear, bare feet silent through the house and into the mud with nothing but a headtorch. Onto the coast path, fast as an arrow through a forest. Brambles unzip the blood from my shins.

On Vault Beach, no rescue boat, no Chinese lantern. The beam of light has gone. The sheep mob crowds the beach like a cloud of unshed rain. The sea is already sweeping in behind the stony ridge in front of the shore, ready to cut them off. Unaware of the trap of the tide, they loot the beach of its seaweed. Their eyes blossom under the moon as they gorge themselves, starving. Streamers of kelp decorate their blissful jaws and the midges cloud their broad dog-faces. The wind shakes their ears like fists. It had not been a longing for another home or a loathing of this one that drove them into the sea, but hunger alone.

The beam of light swings off the cliff again. I angle my own headtorch onto the cliff edge. There's someone up on Dodman's Point. A woman on the edge in a headscarf. A woman with skirts bunched in one hand, shoes in the other.

You're here. Leonela, you're here.

The headscarf is bound around your face and your coat wrapped like a chrysalis around the chaos of your body, and in that moment, I realise you're too close to the edge of the cliff, much too close, your bare toes over the edge, crouching slightly as if preparing to jump but scared to fall. While I'm running up the coast path I imagine you falling, seeing a whip of hair, a bare foot against the night sky. I scream your name but the wind rips my voice away. Sea air summersaults from my throat. Lung-defeated, I reach you in time. Grabbing two fistfuls of your coat, I throw you back onto the coast path, and you stumble but somehow stay on your feet before I barrel into you and fell us both like dried-out trees. I'm on top of you, your body real on mine, warm, warm, no longer dreamlike, you're heaving to take a breath and I rip your hood down and your name tumbles deliciously from my throat –

"Leonela!"

And you're saying *Ruby* back to me but you're angry. You're not embracing me but trapping my arm, which is broken again, beneath the boulder of your body. A twist of hair escapes your hood. Stiff and bleached, not black. A rainstorm of eyeliner. Warm sobs that smell of Frosty Jack's. A bull ring above the raised herring bone of a scar. Arms that cling onto me as if we're both drowning. Suddenly – Leonela – you are not infinitely close. It is Harper who has stolen me and rendered you a full ocean, a lifetime, a constellation away from me.

The Other Pheasant

At the end of term, Ariel suggested, a little obscurely, a game of backgammon on the balcony before we went home. I bought her a 99 cone. Looking back, it wasn't a good idea. I had to go to the park after school and queue with the day students, shivering in my school uniform, clutching the pound coin Pa had given me to use the payphone in an emergency. The ice-cream started to melt on the walk back to school. I'd asked for strawberry sauce which now ran down my wrist, the cone started to soften in my nervous hand. The flake slid and threatened to shatter on the pavement. Not only that, I hadn't changed my clothes. I balanced the cone precariously in the bathroom sink while I put Mother's mink coat on over my uniform and took off my tie. By the time I climbed the spiral staircase, most of it had melted, and I realised Ariel was probably on another starvation diet where she used balsamic vinegar to smother her hunger.

By the time I got to the balcony Ariel was already there, and I opened my mouth to apologise for the ice-cream when she walked up to me until her face was an inch from my face. She put her hands on my shoulders and I stopped apologising. I remembered the feeling of her mouth imprinted on my face with the warmth of the sun. Then she pushed me. She sent me several steps backwards until I had my back against the stone balustrading.

Then she pushed me over it, and I didn't think to push back, I just tumbled over the balustrade, two storeys down onto the paving stones below. My arms shattered up to the elbow and my face bounced off the stones as I landed, splattering ice-cream over Mother's mink coat.

The first thing I heard was Sister Shiloh screaming. I rolled over to see her clutching her cheeks as she shrieked orders at the students who gathered, white-faced, in a wide circle around me. While girls, crying hard, gave up their own school jumpers to be wrapped around my head, Sister Shiloh asked someone to fetch my dolly from the dormitory so I would have it with me in the hospital. It was Renxiang who raced down two flights of stairs, carrying Resusci-Anne under her good arm.

Sister Shiloh drove me to the hospital in the passenger seat of the headteacher's car, and she kept taking her eyes off the road to sob at the way blood dotted fast into my lap in spite of the jumpers bound around my head. If I had owned a Pink Jubilee Barbie, I would have clutched it tightly. Instead, Resusci-

Anne lay across the backseat, freckled with five years of balsamic vinegar, gazing indifferently.

I remember all of this clearly: I can even recall numbness spreading to my fingertips as I was hoisted off of the paving stones by my underarms. I remember my feet getting cold as my shoes came off on the wet stones. I remember begging Renxiang to let the warbler out of our dormitory, and Renxiang shaking her head through her tears as my voice tumbled like wind and rain through a window, failing to form words.

But just as dreams do not let us hit the ground nor do memories, so in the moment of falling from the balcony I'm not myself at all, but instead watching myself from behind the balustrade, thrown up improbably into the air and then tumbling like a broken pheasant into an ocean, ribbons of blood leaping pre-emptively from my sides like a fanfare. A small 'oh' of surprise knocked from my lungs, the feeling of Ariel's mouth on my face lost as the mean, pinched sky turns over, once, twice, three times overhead.

The Refugees

Irma is dead. The bag of fudge that I bought myself is limp in my hand as I stare at the telly. She died in the night. Her doctor at Great Ormond Street is saying her endurance of injury should be an inspiration to us all, and that she died peacefully in her sleep after developing septic shock from bacteraemia. He says that she had learned to speak perfect English. There's a photo of her in a wheelchair in the hospital classroom, reading 'Alice through the Looking Glass'. When lambs develop septic shock there's no saving them, they're often gone within the same night. I wonder if someone took Irma outside near the end. I wonder if anyone spoke to her in Bosnian.

After the night with Harper on Dodman's Point, Pa drove me to the hospital himself after spending an hour swearing and fiddling under the bonnet of his jeep. He demanded that the doctor change my Tramadol for something else, and the doctor struggled visibly while he told her I'd been behaving like a *bleddy tuss*, but while he complained about me I was stunned to hear him say your name. The doctor nodded and said that there was a risk of Tramadol causing delusions, even delirium, especially in children. She told Pa to buy me standard painkillers from the pharmacy.

Now John Major is on the telly, saying that the first Bosnian refugees are being welcomed at Stansted airport today, that they will all be provided with six-month visas. Not in dinghies, not washed up onto Cornish beaches. You are absent from my dreams and I am further from you than ever.

Live footage shows clusters of young men coming through the automatic doors at the airport. They hold hands as if preparing to be pulled from one another. One of them smiles nervously into the camera, bowing his head as if shy and grateful at the same time. Another weeps, one hand pressed over his eye. Chains of volunteers pass them sandwiches, paper cups of tea, Ziplock bags of soap and toothpaste. Children hold signs that say:

DOBRODOŠLI IZBJEGLICE
WELCOME REFUGEES

You are not moving around the edges of the world alone and I do not have to think of lightning that falls into the sea around you. You will not arrive with something as unpredictable as the wind, but to a city that is far from here, warm and well-practiced. Familiar language. Tea without milk, the way you are used to it.

At home, in the binbag of exercise books from school, I find the clip frame with Ariel's photo, which Sister Shiloh would have thought was mine. Ariel, young and spinning with her hair and dress whirling. I take her photo out and throw it away, replacing it with the newspaper photo of you. I wish I had another photo of you – if only the journalist had taken one more. One where you are not quite so sad. One where I can see your face, and your hands look less perfectly small.

I unfold the paku-paku I made for you. There are two blank squares left but I'm out of questions.

Nedostajala si mi. Close to the English for 'I miss you': *you are missing from me.*

Mesačekaću. A single word to say *I will wait for you here.*

An End to Drowning

I pour butterscotch syrup around the inside of a glass and add sheep's milk from the bottle, first flicking the plug of butterfat into the bin with a teaspoon.

"Sorry it's warm," I say, handing Harper the glass. She smells of the ocean after spending the morning pushing wheelbarrows of seaweed from the beach to the paddocks, spreading armloads of it around for the sheep to chew steadily and ignore the gate that she forgets to close. She's brought a watermelon for the black face lamb, who she has named Little My. She feeds him pieces as he balances on his hind legs, pink splashing down his front, and butts her with his lumpy skull, a need that could almost be mistaken for love. Late-blooming zinnias sit in the vase on the table, almost too bright for the kitchen.

School settled the lawsuit out of court. The lawyer wanted to negotiate further, said we could get twice as much, but I declined, finding the whole process humiliating. It was more than enough to build a new barn, and the mob is growing fast now that we bring seaweed up for the sheep and they're not driven, by hunger, to the sea. I paid to get mother's coat cleaned and then sold it. I wrote a cheque for the rest of the settlement to the address on the fundraising campaign that your picture was on. The secretariat from the Refugee Council sent me a personal letter.

"Ruby, which colour?" Harper asks, my paku-paku on her fingers.

"Blue."

"B-L-U-E." She snaps the paku-paku back and forth. "Number?"

"Two."

"One-two." She lifts the fold of paper to read a question about secrets. I risk telling her about shooting one of her mum's pheasants in the hope that she might find it funny. She throws her head back with a great shout of laughter, louder than I expected, says next time I should eat it. She sweeps a finger round her empty glass to suck the remnants of syrup, then cups Little My's quivering face and snuffles deeply into his neck. There's a lovely greed in everything she does.

"So, what happened with your accident?" she asks eventually, the paku-paku already forgotten on the table. It's the first time she's mentioned it.

"Tug of war got out of hand."

She smiles and waits.

"Not sure. Maybe no reason. This girl didn't like me very much. Girls tend not to like me."

"Want me to murder her? I'll do it. I'll push her off Dodman's Point." And there it is: the moment I think she might tell me. Instead she stares into her glass, empty except for a kiss of white along its rim. "Sorry about breaking your arm." Barely audible. Humiliation radiates off her in the electric silence.

"It's ok. I'm pretty sure I broke it when I shot the pheasant." I force a laugh so she'll hear it without looking up. I remember how Mrs T said Harper had trouble written all over her, but it's not trouble, only hurt that's written through and through. I'm making it sound shit, sitting in a kitchen that smells of seaweed, drinking warm milkshakes and embarrassing ourselves. But it's not shit. It's perfect.

"It wasn't the first time I ... I went up there. To the cliff edge," she says.

I thought I had saved her by some heroic coincidence.

"No, I guessed."

I'm trying to decide whether it's ok to say I hoped it would be the last time. I imagine the words hanging in the air and how they will sound. Whether they will be humiliating like a headteacher, hectoring and ungenerous like Ariel, or off-putting in a more indefinable way.

Harper jumps up and suggests swimming before the sun goes down. I realise the silence was probably becoming embarrassing. She's out the door in an instant and I'm fumbling behind her, annoyed with myself, and she's kicking off her boots, shedding clothes as she sprints to the beach with Little My bucking alongside her. I pick up her clothes as I follow, worrying about the tide. Harper tries to call Little My to play in the shallows, but he shies away, lies down on the warm sand. One side of his face droops under his empty eye socket. Harper stoops to kiss him and as she does, she covers one side of her face with her hand to match his, but still her kiss escapes from behind it and still laughter rings from her half-a-mouth and echoes off the cliff beneath Dodmans Point, cartwheels back to us. Harper strides into the sea. Just before diving under a wave, she asks what it was like to fall, shouting over the sound of the breaking shore.

I no longer dream that you and I are sheep midwives or naked in a dinghy, or two warblers, or two parts of one warbler cut in half by light. I no longer gaze at the moon-road on the ocean and wait for you. There is no English word for this: for watching Harper dip below each swell and waiting for her to reappear again. It's as though I was on the outside of the world and looking in, pressed up against it, looking for a way into it, but as I inch one foot in the water I'm finding a way in. I follow Harper into the waves. Straws of sunlight dance off her bare shoulders. It's in no imagined language or reality, but this one, that the current sweeps my feet from the seabed and I vibrate as if brought to life by the cold water, trying to keep her within my sight. The warblers are gone for the autumn, so I don't think of how much or little I feel like them. Only this human purpose - to be here when the cold becomes too much and Harper turns to swim back to a beach where someone is waiting.

About the Author

Ellie has a BA from the University of Chichester Thompson Rivers University (CA), an MA from Bath  Spa University and a PhD from University of Plymouth. She has had short fiction and poetry published with journals in Canada, India, Nepal and the UK. Ellie wrote a play called 'A Patient Drug' which was produced and performed in Cornwall and at Royal Holloway University, and she was an Associate Editor for the travel writing journal Coldnoon Travel Poetics, where she wrote a column on South Asian literature. Her debut novella-in-flash 'Birds with Horse Hearts' won the Bath Flash Fiction Award in 2019, and was shortlisted for a Saboteur Award. When Ellie isn't writing she can be found crawling through the long grasses of the Nepalese jungle, getting regrettably close to the local one-horned rhinos.